GRAPHIC SHAKESPEARE
ROMEO & JULIET

CONTENTS

Published by
Evans Brothers Limited
2A Portman Mansions
Chiltern Street
London W1M 1LE

© in the modern text Hilary Burningham 1997
© in the illustrations Evans Brothers Ltd 1997
Designed by Design Systems Ltd.

British Library Cataloguing in Publication Data
Burningham, Hilary
  Romeo and Juliet
  Teacher's book. – (The graphic Shakespeare series)
  1. Shakespeare, William, 1564-1616. Romeo and Juliet
  2. Shakespeare, William, 1564-1616 – Study and teaching
  (Secondary)
  I. Title II. Fripp, Emily
  822.3'3

ISBN 0 237 51794 9

Printed in Hong Kong by Wing King Tong Co. Ltd.

INTRODUCTION TO
THE GRAPHIC ROMEO AND JULIET ACTIVITY BOOK

The play and its themes

Romeo and Juliet will probably strike more common chords with the modern teenager than any other Shakespeare play! Family rows, domestic violence, gang warfare – is this "Eastenders"? No, it's *Romeo and Juliet*. The themes are as relevant today as they were four hundred years ago. And youthful passions and emotions are as earth-moving now as they were in Elizabethan England. As educators, we will want to help our students to discover the striking similarities between themes in the play and events in their own lives. We will want to use every means to open up the treasure chest of Shakespeare's drama and use of language. The adapted text and the activities in this book are intended to point students in the direction of some of the key themes in the play. The extent to which these themes are brought out more explicitly will depend on the ability level and interests of the students. As they work through the activities, students should become aware that:

- *love and hate are both powerful emotions.* Tybalt's hatred and constant, simmering rage contrast with the theme of Romeo and Juliet's unfolding love story.
- *no one knows what love is like until they actually experience it.* Romeo's and Juliet's early ideas about love are different from the reality of their feelings for each other.
- *love can cause conflicts within the family and with society.* Formerly obedient young people can become outright rebels when they are in the grip of this powerful emotion.

The "star-crossed lovers" theme is referred to in the Prologue (see *Appendix 1, page 31*), and also in the analysis of Friar Laurence's complicated plan (see page 26). The analysis is intended to show that a successful outcome depends very much on the co-ordination of events over which neither he nor Romeo and Juliet have very much control. Juliet, who has great intelligence and imagination, contemplates the risks before taking the sleeping potion.

It is not suggested that every student should complete every activity in the book. Rather it is the intention to provide manageable tasks at each stage of the play so that the teacher has available suitable materials for the students who need them. An added bonus is that a student notebook or file containing a selection of completed activities provides a good framework for revision.

The student activities

The majority of the activities provided in the photocopiable book are sufficiently straightforward to enable any student to work independently and produce a respectable piece of work. In some activities, sentences are provided for completion; in others, questions are closely matched to the text to facilitate the student response. The advantage of this very basic approach is that it helps pupils to become accustomed to correct usage. At a certain stage in language development, particularly for those using English as a second or other language, struggling with open questions may lead to the reinforcement of past mistakes, or to frustration when trying to produce original writing without having acquired the skills to do so. There are a number of suggestions and opportunities for more demanding work where it is appropriate. In some activities, the student (or the teacher) can choose between a challenging or a straightforward task.

There can be no substitute for the excitement of a Shakespeare play performed live on stage. *The Graphic Shakespeare* aims to make his work more accessible to readers representing various cultural backgrounds and levels of ability in the hope that they will be encouraged to explore further, developing their appreciation and new skills in the process.

Attainment levels

In keeping with the aims of the National Curriculum, and to promote effective monitoring and record-keeping in line with the Special Needs Code of Practice, appropriate attainment levels are suggested for each activity. It should be noted that in general the attainment levels given for Reading (Attainment Target 2: AT2) are higher than those for Writing (AT 3). This is because Shakespeare's text, even with the aids and prompts that are given, demands a good level of reading comprehension. Keeping in mind that AT 2 emphasises responses to a range of texts, the work on Shakespeare needs to be seen as part of the balanced selection of literature that the pupil will study in the course of the year. Understanding Shakespeare's language will contribute to the pupil's attaining up to Level 5. Higher levels in AT 3 can be achieved by opting for the more challenging tasks.

Speaking and listening

Given the National Curriculum emphasis on Speaking and Listening (AT 1), students are encouraged to work with a partner or in small groups whenever possible in order to promote verbal and aural skills, particularly in the art of reading/speaking Shakespeare's language. Other activities that promote both discussion and an element of peer group teaching are: *Desktop Teaching* (page 42) and the *"Who Am I?"* package (pages 37-41) that includes Character Clue cards and rules for the game. These are excellent revision techniques, once the students have an overview of the play. The Character Clues can be used in several ways. First, in preparation for the *"Who Am I?"* game, portraits from the Picture Gallery need to be matched to the cards. In a turnaround, the portraits alone may be placed on the cards, with pupils writing their own sets of 'clues'. Similarly, portraits can be matched with Key Speeches, under the heading of *"Who Said That?"*.

The Key Speeches

The Key Speeches that appear in the Graphic text and on a number of activity sheets have two main functions. First, to help students gain an understanding of and a feeling for Shakespeare's language. Second, to provide an opportunity to speak Shakespeare's lines in small, manageable sections. Key Speeches featured in the Activities and in the Appendices, mostly appear with the original text beside a modern, paraphrased version. Students may experiment with the dialogue in modern English before moving to Shakespeare's English. The two texts provide a useful introduction to paraphrasing, an old-fashioned but extremely useful technique. Eventually, some students may enjoy doing their own paraphrasing.

The idea of mime is introduced as the first activity (page 5), to promote the use of actions and gestures as part of the acting process. It is also effective as a loosening-up technique to encourage students to get involved in the drama. They should be encouraged to use large, sweeping gestures – even at the expense of feeling a bit daft in front of their peers! Students will often need to be reminded of the importance of how they move on the stage. Suggestions of other scenes appropriate for mime have been included.

Radio Newsroom Verona

National Curriculum requirements to study different aspects of the media can offer exciting opportunities. The device of the Radio Newsroom is used here because it provides an immediate and vivid way to show the impact of the Montague-Capulet feud on the wider population. A suggested script is given. The language is not difficult, giving practice in reading to approximately Level 3. Further eyewitness accounts or ongoing hourly bulletins provide additional scope for original writing. Students can be encouraged to imitate the characteristics of newsroom presentation as in the example.

If your school has a video camera, this could, of course, become *T.V. Newsroom Verona*.

The student record sheet

The student record sheet (*Record of My Work*, page 47) provides an all-important opportunity for self-assessment. The student enters the number and titles of the sheet, together with an indication of how well it was completed. The student then assesses the degree of ease or difficulty of each activity. If he or she is ticking too many 'easy' boxes, it is clearly time to move to more challenging work. There is a final column for teacher comment.

Students are also encouraged, on completion of the unit on *Romeo and Juliet*, to assess and comment on the outcomes on the sheet *What Things Have Improved?* on page 48.

STARTING A FIGHT

Work in groups of four. Choose who will be Gregory and Sampson, the Capulets.
Choose who will be Abram and the other servant, who are Montagues. First, mime this scene,
which means acting it out without speaking - you should not make any sounds at all!
Second, try acting it using modern English. Finally, use Shakespeare's English (*on Worksheet 1.2*). It is very
short. Try to say the words from memory. Once you have mimed it, actions only, continue to use the actions
while speaking the words. Decide which part of the classroom is to be your stage. Move the furniture out of
the way so that you can do all the actions.

Mime

Gregory and Sampson are on one side of the stage. Abram and the other servant come in at the other side.
Gregory and Sampson nudge each other and wave their swords. Sampson walks over to the Montagues and
walks up and down biting his thumb – he clicks his thumb against his top teeth, flicking his thumb outwards.
This was a very rude gesture in Shakespeare's time. He walks in a very cocky way. He is "winding up" Abram and
the other servant. He wants to start a fight! Gregory sees another Capulet coming. He points offstage. Now
Gregory and Sampson feel brave. They start to attack Abram and the other servant. Abram and the other servant
get out their swords. They all fight.

Here is what they say, in modern English:

GREGORY: *I will frown as I walk past them. They can take it how they like.*

SAMPSON: *I'm going to bite my thumb at them. They should be ashamed if they put up
with that.*
(Sampson makes a big point of walking up and down in front of Abram and the other (Montague)
servant, flicking his thumb on his teeth)

ABRAM: *Are you biting your thumb at us?*

SAMPSON: *I'm biting my thumb.*

ABRAM: *Are you biting your thumb at us?*

SAMPSON:
(talking to Gregory) *Is the law on our side if I say "Yes"?*

GREGORY: *No.*

SAMPSON: *I'm not biting my thumb at you.
But I am biting my thumb.*

GREGORY: *Do you want to fight?*

ABRAM: *Fight? No, I don't want to.*

SAMPSON: *If you do want a fight, I'll fight
with you. My master is as good as yours.*

ABRAM: *Your master is no better than mine.*

GREGORY: (sees another Capulet coming; he points offstage)
You can say our master is better. Here comes one of our people.

SAMPSON: *My master is better!*

ABRAM: *You're lying!*

SAMPSON: *Draw your swords, if you're men. Gregory, remember your slashing blow.*

They all fight.

AT 2: Level 2-4

STARTING A FIGHT (continued)

Now try Shakespeare's language

(Gregory and Sampson are on the stage, to one side. Abram and another servant enter from the other side. Gregory and Sampson look at them angrily.)

GREGORY:	I will frown as I pass by, and let them take it as they list.
SAMPSON:	I will bite my thumb at them; which is disgrace to them if they bear it. (Sampson walks up and down in front of Abram and the other servant.)
ABRAM:	Do you bite your thumb at us, sir?
SAMPSON:	I do bite my thumb, sir.
ABRAM:	Do you bite your thumb at us, sir?
SAMPSON: (aside to Gregory)	Is the law of our side if I say 'Ay'?
GREGORY: (aside to Sampson)	No.
SAMPSON:	No, sir, I do not bite my thumb at you, sir. But I bite my thumb, sir
GREGORY:	Do you quarrel, sir?
ABRAM:	Quarrel, sir? No, sir.
SAMPSON:	But if you do, sir, I am for you. I serve as good a man as you.
ABRAM:	No better.
GREGORY: (aside to Sampson)	Say better. Here comes one of my master's kinsmen.
SAMPSON:	Yes, better, sir.
ABRAM:	You lie.
SAMPSON:	Draw, if you be men. Gregory, remember your slashing blow.
	They fight.

> When you have tried the miming, and acted out the speeches, work with your group
> to complete the following in your notebook.

1. There were two families, the _____ and the _____.

2. They lived in a city called _____ in _____.

3. They _____ each other.

4. Even the _____ would fight.

5. In this scene, two Capulet servants, _____ and _____ , met two _____
    servants. One of the Montague servants was called _____.

6. It was very rude to bite your _____ at someone else.

AT 2: Level 2-4

CAPULETS AND MONTAGUES

Read page 6 of your *Graphic Romeo and Juliet*. You have now met some of the characters in the play. It will be important to keep track of which family each character belongs to. On a separate page in your notebook, make three columns. Write **Capulets** at the top of one column, **Montagues** at the top of the next, and **Neither** at the top of the third. It should look like the example below. Write the names of the characters in the play so far under the correct heading. As you read the story and the play, you can add to your list.

Capulets	Montagues	Neither

You should have the following characters on your list:

Old Capulet	Old Montague	Tybalt	Benvolio	The Prince
Gregory	Abram	Sampson	another servant	

Working with a partner, write the answers to the following questions in your notebook. Make sure that your answers are in good sentences. The first one is done as an example.

1. Who tried to stop the fighting? What family was he from?

    Benvolio tried to stop the fighting. He was a Montague.

2. Who picked a fight with Benvolio? What family was he from?

3. What did the heads of the two families want to do?

4. Who tried to stop them?

Key Speeches

Here are two important speeches. With a partner, read them in modern English, then in Shakespeare's English. Benvolio would be shouting above the noise of the fighting. Remember that Tybalt really hated all the Montagues. Try to make him sound full of hate.

BENVOLIO:	I do but keep the peace. Put up thy sword, Or manage it to part these men with me.	*I'm trying to stop this fight. Put your sword away,* *or use it to help me separate these men.*
TYBALT:	What, drawn, and talk of peace? I hate the word As I hate hell, all Montagues, and thee. Have at thee, coward!	*You have your sword out, yet you talk of peace? I hate that word* *as much as I hate hell. And I hate all Montagues and I hate you.* *I'll fight you, you coward.*

AT 3:2-3

THE PRINCE WAS ANGRY

Working with a partner, write the answers to the following questions in your notebook. Remember that your answers should be written in good sentences. You will find the answers to the questions on page 8 of *The Graphic Romeo and Juliet*.

1.   Who was the ruler of Verona?

2.   Why was he angry?

3.   Why were the people of Verona carrying weapons?

4.   What was the punishment for the next person who started a fight?

Choose a headline

Pretend to be a newspaper reporter in Verona in the time of *Romeo and Juliet*. From the list of headlines, choose one – or write your own. Then, either write a newspaper story about the fighting and what the Prince said, or read the sentences below and put them into the correct order.

"I'VE HAD ENOUGH!" SAYS PRINCE

"THIS BRAWLING HAS GOT TO STOP!"

DEATH TO THOSE WHO START BRAWLS

DANGER WALKS VERONA'S STREETS!

FEUDING¹ FAMILIES OUT OF CONTROL

Write the News Story

Lord Capulet and Lord Montague were seen shouting at each other. He said that the fighting must stop.

The fighting broke out between servants.

Death would be the punishment for the next person who started a fight.

Prince Escalus hurried to the place.

Another brawl broke out today between the Montagues and the Capulets.

Soon members of the two families joined in.

¹feuding – always fighting

AT 3: 2-5

ROMEO WAS UNHAPPY

Other people talked about Romeo before he came into the story. Below are some sentences about him. Working with a partner, decide what you learned about Romeo on page 10.

Learned on page 10	Yes	No
1. Romeo was always unhappy.		
2. Romeo could ride a horse.		
3. He was the son of Lord and Lady Montague.		
4. Romeo was a farmer.		
5. He was Benvolio's cousin.		
6. Everyone was worried about him.		

Working with a partner, talk about the following sentences.
Choose the correct word from the brackets and write the sentences in your notebook.
Underline the word you have chosen from the brackets.

1. (*Benvolio   Tybalt   Lady Capulet*) was a troublemaker.

2. Romeo was the Montagues' (*nephew   uncle   son*).

3. Romeo was always (*sad   happy   angry*).

4. Benvolio was Romeo's (*nephew   uncle   cousin*).

5. Benvolio wanted to find out why Romeo was so (*silly   brave   unhappy*).

6. Benvolio was very (*understanding   annoying   bad-tempered*).

7. Romeo was in (*trouble   love   difficulty*).

8. The lady Romeo loved had vowed never to love any (*flower   tree   man*)

9. Benvolio said that Romeo should get to know other (*people   ladies   children*).

10. Romeo was sure that he could never (*love   like   hate*) anyone else.

Now, make up other sentences with words to choose from. Try them out on your partner.

Example:

Tybalt was a (*Montague   Smith   Capulet*).

ROMEO

AT 3: 1-3

JULIET
A Very Important Person

> Other people talked about Juliet before she came into the story.
> Work with a partner, and ask each other the following questions:

1. What was the name of the Capulets' daughter?
2. Whom did the County Paris want to marry?
3. Who was fourteen years old?
4. Who was too young to be married?
5. Who would Paris see at the Capulets' party that night?

The list of guests

> Look at page 16 of *The Graphic Romeo and Juliet*. Find the answers to the following questions.
> Write the answers in your notebook. Remember to use good sentences.

1. Old Capulet's servant had a problem about the list of guests. What was the problem?
2. Who helped the servant with the list?
3. What was the name of the lady Romeo loved?
4. Was she invited to the party?
5. Were there any Montague names on the list?
6. Why not?
7. Why did the servant invite Romeo and Benvolio to the party?
8. What was Benvolio's good idea?

> Here is the list of guests. Practise reading the list, enjoying the Italian names. You may need help in
> pronouncing some of them. If you enjoy doing fancy writing, write the list on a scroll.

Signor Martino and his wife and daughters.

County Anselm and his beauteous sister.

The lady widow of Utruvio.

Signor Placentio and his lovely nieces.

Mercutio and his brother Valentine.

Mine uncle Capulet, his wife, and daughters.

My fair niece Rosaline and Livia.

Signor Valentio and his cousin Tybalt.

Lucio and the lively Helena.

AT 3: 2-3 AT 1: 2-3

JULIET'S IDEAS ABOUT LOVE

Key Speeches

With a partner, read the following speeches. Juliet is quiet, and wants to please her parents.

	Shakespeare's English	***Modern English***
LADY CAPULET:	What say you? Can you love the gentleman? This night you shall behold him at our feast. Read o'er the volume of young Paris' face, And find delight writ there with beauty's pen. Speak briefly, can you like of Paris' love?	*What do you think? Could you love Paris? You'll see him at the party tonight. Look at him carefully, as if you were reading a book; You will like what you see. Answer me quickly, do you like the idea of Paris loving you?*
JULIET:	I'll look to like, if looking liking move. But no more deep will I endart mine eye Than your consent gives strength to make it fly.	*I shall expect to like him, and I probably will like him. But I will only let myself love him if you, my parents, want me to love him.*

Look at page 18 in your *Graphic Romeo and Juliet*. Then, talk about the sentences below and choose the best answer. Write the sentences in your notebook.

1. Juliet hadn't thought about marriage, because
   – she didn't want to marry at all.
   – she was only fourteen years old.

2. Juliet wanted to
   – choose her own husband
   – do as her parents wished
   – stay single.

3. About Paris, Juliet's feeling was that
   – she could never love him.
   – he would be very boring.
   – she would like him if her parents wanted her to.

4. Juliet seemed to think that love was a feeling that
   – she could turn on and off.
   – could get out of control.

JULIET

• Don't forget to put the Nurse on your list of Capulets.

AT 2: 2-5

ROMEO'S IDEAS ABOUT LOVE

With a partner, or in groups, talk about Romeo's ideas about love.
Remember that he was in love with Rosaline, who had sworn[1] never to love a man. He had nothing to
be happy about. He was going to the Capulets' party with Mercutio and Benvolio. He expected to
be miserable. Read the Key Speeches below and talk about his feelings about love.

Key Speeches

	Shakespeare's English	*Modern English*
ROMEO: (to Mercutio)	You have dancing shoes With nimble soles. I have a soul of lead So stakes me to the ground I cannot move.	*You are happy –* *you can dance and enjoy yourself. My* *insides feel heavy as lead, as if I'm tied to* *the ground and can't move.*
MERCUTIO:	You are a lover. Borrow Cupid's[2] wings And soar with them above a common bound.	*You're in love. You should be flying high* *on the wings of love.*
ROMEO:	Under love's heavy burden I do sink. Is love a tender thing? It is too rough, Too rude, too boisterous, and it pricks like thorn.	*My love is like a heavy weight, crushing me.* *Is love gentle and kind? No, it is rough,* *unkind, violent and painful as a sharp* *thorn on a bush.*

In your notebooks, write the title, Romeo's Ideas About Love. Choose the words
from the list below that fit Romeo's ideas about love and use them to finish the sentence,
Romeo though that love was _____.

Romeo thought that love was _____ _____ _____ _____.

light   sad   beautiful   romantic

gloomy   painful   happy   rough

wonderful   heavy   violent   unkind   gentle

ROMEO

[1]sworn – made a solemn promise to God
[2]Cupid – Cupid was the god of love; he is shown as a baby with wings

AT 3: 2-5

LOVE AT FIRST SIGHT

Romeo's speech when he first saw Juliet is probably one of the most famous speeches
in Shakespeare. It's worth studying, speaking aloud, and memorising. Work with a partner and try
the modern English, then Shakespeare's English. It's worth the effort.

Key Speech

ROMEO:

O, she doth teach the torches to burn bright!
It seems she hangs upon the cheek of night
As a rich jewel in an Ethiop's ear –
Beauty too rich for use, for earth too dear!
So shows a snowy dove trooping with crows
As yonder lady o'er her fellows shows.
The measure done, I'll watch her place of stand
And, touching hers, make blessed my rude hand.
Did my heart love till now? Forswear it, sight!
For I ne'er saw true beauty till this night.

*She can teach the torches how to burn
brightly.*
She's a blazing jewel against dark skin.
She's too beautiful for everyday life.
*She's like a beautiful white bird among
dark crows.*
*When the dance is finished, I'll watch to see
where she goes,*
and I'll dare to touch her hand.
Was I in love before now? No!
I have never seen real beauty until tonight.

(Romeo would say this speech in a quiet, amazed way.)

Try to say the speech from memory. If possible, tape-record some of the best readings.

AT 3: 3-5

TYBALT'S HATE

This is a very angry scene between Tybalt and Capulet. Act it out with a partner. You are both wanting to shout, but you have to keep your voices down. You don't want the other guests to hear you. The speeches should be spoken quite quickly. Some of them have been shortened to help you. When you have practised the scene, perform it for the class. Do you like using Shakespeare's English or modern English? Why?

	Shakespeare's English	**Modern English**
TYBALT:	This, by his voice, should be a Montague. Fetch me my rapier, boy. Now, by the stock and honour of my kin, To strike him dead I hold it not a sin.	*This fellow sounds like a Montague. Bring me my sword. Now for the honour of our family it would be no sin to kill him now.*
CAPULET:	Why, how now, kinsman? Wherefore storm you so?	*Why are you so angry?*
TYBALT:	Uncle, this is a Montague, our foe.	*Uncle, this is a Montague, our enemy.*
CAPULET:	Young Romeo is it?	*Is it young Romeo?*
TYBALT:	'Tis he, that villain Romeo.	*It's him, the wicked Romeo.*
CAPULET:	Content thee, gentle coz, let him alone. 'A bears him like a portly gentleman. It is my will, the which if thou respect, Show a fair presence and put off these frowns, An ill-beseeming semblance for a feast.	*Relax, nephew, leave him alone. He looks alright to me. I should like you to do as I wish-- be friendly to people and don't be angry. It's not right to be angry at a party.*
TYBALT:	It fits when such a villain is a guest. I'll not endure him.	*It's right to be angry when such a bad man is a guest. I'll not put up with it.*
CAPULET:	(loses his temper) He shall be endured. What, goodman boy! I say he shall. Go to! Am I the master here, or you? Go to! You'll not endure him! God shall mend my soul! You'll make a mutiny among my guests! You will set cock-a-hoop! You'll be the man!	*You will put up with it. You youngster! I say he shall stay. Stop it! Am I the boss around here or you? Stop it! You'll not put up with him! God help us! You'll start a fight among my guests? You'll get it going? You think you're a big man around here?*
TYBALT:	Why, uncle, 'tis a shame.	*Uncle, this brings shame on our family.*
CAPULET:	Be quiet, or ---- ------ For shame! I'll make you quiet!	*Shut up, or I will make you shut up.*
TYBALT:	(Tybalt goes away, very angry) I will withdraw. But this intrusion shall, Now seeming sweet, convert to bitterest gall.	*I'm leaving. What has happened may seem alright to you, but very bad things will come of it.*

Tybalt's Rage

When you have acted the scene, answer the questions below. Remember to use good sentences.

1. Who recognised Romeo?
2. What did Tybalt want to do to Romeo?
3. What did Old Capulet say?
4. What did old Capulet do when Tybalt wouldn't shut up?
5. What did Tybalt say as he left? (Write Shakespeare's words.)

AT 2: 2-5
AT 3: 2-3

FALLING IN LOVE

This is about Romeo and Juliet's first meeting. First, write about it from Romeo's side, then from Juliet's side. The sentences below will help you, or you may prefer to write it in your own words.

Romeo's side

I went to the _____ ball. I really went along just to please my friends _____ and

_____ .

Then I saw her! I didn't know _____ she was. She was the most _____ girl I had ever seen.
She seemed brighter than the _____ . She was _____ with someone else.

After the dance, I stood _____ her. All I wanted was to touch her _____ . When I touched her
hand, I wanted to kiss her. We kissed, and we kissed _____ .

I asked an old _____ who the girl was. She was the daughter of Lord and Lady _____ !
This was _____ news.

Capulets'   Mercutio   Benvolio   who
beautiful   torches   dancing   beside   hand
again   woman   Capulet   terrible

Juliet's side

My parents had put on a wonderful _____ . Everyone in _____ came. I was going to get to
know _____ . He wants to marry me.

Suddenly, there was a young man standing _____ me. He took my _____ . He said he wanted to
kiss me. I felt _____ at first. Then I couldn't _____ myself. We kissed _____ .

I liked this young man a lot. I asked the _____ who he was. His name was _____ . He was
the only son of the _____ family, our great _____!

ball   Verona   Paris   beside
hand   shy   stop   again
Nurse   Romeo   Montague   enemies

ROMEO   JULIET

AT 3: 2

AFTER THE BALL

After the ball at the Capulets, Romeo didn't want to go home with his friends.
He wanted to see Juliet again. He hid from his friends. These sentences tell what happened next.
Can you put them in the correct order? Talk about it with a partner, then write the sentences
in your notebooks. Page 26 in your *Graphic Romeo and Juliet* will help you.

Jumbled sentences:

He couldn't hide any longer.

They wanted to be married.

Juliet came out onto the balcony.

They talked about their love. They were very, very happy.

Romeo hid from his friends.

Juliet said that she loved Romeo.

Juliet spoke aloud. She talked about her feelings for Romeo.

Romeo went to see Friar Laurence.

He spoke to Juliet.

Romeo was very happy when he heard Juliet say that she loved him.

Key Speeches

Read these speeches with a partner. Juliet is on a balcony and Romeo on the ground. They can hear
and see each other, but can't touch. They have to speak quietly because Juliet's family and servants would kill
Romeo if they knew he was near their house. You will find a longer version of this scene in the Appendix.

JULIET: (she is speaking aloud; she doesn't know that Romeo is
           listening)
           Romeo, doff thy name;
           And for thy name which is no part of thee,
           Take all myself.

(She is speaking aloud. She thinks she is alone.)

Romeo, get rid of your name,
and instead of your name, which isn't part of
you anyway,
have me in place of your name.

ROMEO: (he is so happy, he has to speak to her)
           I take thee at thy word.
           Call me but love, and I'll be new baptized.
           Henceforth I never will be Romeo.

(he is so happy to hear what she says, he has to speak
to her)
I'll take you at your word.
If you love me, I'll take a new name.
I shan't be Romeo from now on.

JULIET: (she is surprised to hear his voice)
           What man art thou that, thus bescreened in
           night,
           So stumblest on my counsel?

(She didn't know anyone was listening to her. She is
surprised.)
Who are you, hiding in the dark,
Listening to what I am saying?

ROMEO: By a name
           I know not how to tell thee who I am.
           My name, dear saint, is hateful to myself
           Because it is an enemy to thee.
           Had I it written, I would tear the word.

I don't know how to tell you who I am.
My name is the name of your enemy and
so I hate it.
If it was written on paper, I would rip it up.

AT 2: Level 2-5
AT 3: Level 2

FRIAR LAURENCE

> Read page 28 of *The Graphic Shakespeare*, and look at the picture on page 29.
> Read the sentences below, and write them in your notebook, filling in the spaces.

FRIAR LAURENCE

1. In those days, priests were like _____ .

2. They looked after _____ people.

3. Medicines were made from _____ .

4. Plants could make people _____ or

    they could make people _____ .

5. Friar Laurence knew all about these _____ .

Friar Laurence had a surprise

> Look at page 30 in *The Graphic Romeo and Juliet*. Answer the following questions
> in your notebooks. Remember to write in good sentences.

1. What did Romeo tell Friar Laurence?

2. Why was Friar Laurence surprised?

3. Why did Friar Laurence agree to marry Romeo and Juliet?

> With a partner or in groups, look at the question below. Talk about it, and write a short answer in your own
> words. Read your answer to the class.

Friar Laurence agreed to marry Romeo and Juliet. Do you think he was right?

AT 2: 3
AT 3: 2-4

ROMEO'S PLANS

Key Speech

ROMEO:　　Bid her devise　　　　　　　　　　　*Tell her to find a way*
　　　　　　Some means to come to shrift¹ this afternoon,　*to come to confession² this afternoon*
　　　　　　And there she shall at Friar Laurence' cell　*And there at Friar Laurence's*
　　　　　　Be shrived and married.　　　　　　　*She will say her confession and be married.*

> Working with a partner, talk about the following questions. Look at page 32 of your *Graphic Romeo and Juliet* to help you. Write the answers in your books. Remember to use good sentences.

1.　Did Benvolio and Mercutio know that Romeo had fallen in love with Juliet?

2.　What were the two messages Romeo gave the Nurse for Juliet?

3.　What reason could Juliet give for going to see Friar Laurence?

4.　What was her real reason for going to see him?

5.　How was Romeo going to get to her bedroom that night?

¹shrift − to tell a priest about the bad things you have done. The priest tells you what you must do to make up for your sins
²confession − the same as shrift

AT 3: 2-3

A SECRET MARRIAGE

Romeo and Juliet were very much in love. They wanted to be together. They wanted to be married. They didn't think about the problems they might have. Below is a list of problems. With a partner, read them and talk about them. Make two columns, and put them under the correct headings. Can you think of other problems they might, or might not, have?

1. They both loved their parents, yet their parents hated each other.

2. They didn't have anywhere to live.

3. Romeo's friends and family were always fighting Juliet's friends and family.

4. There was never enough money.

5. They didn't have much chance to get to know each other.

6. They had to keep their love a secret all the time.

Problems for Romeo and Juliet	Not problems for Romeo and Juliet

ROMEO

JULIET

ANOTHER FIGHT

Look at page 38 in *The Graphic Romeo and Juliet*. With a partner, or in groups, talk about the questions below. In your notebooks, write answers to the questions. Remember to answer in good sentences.

1.   Who tried to make everyone be sensible?

2.   Why didn't Romeo want to fight with Tybalt?

3.   What did Mercutio call Tybalt?

4.   Why was Tybalt able to hurt Mercutio?

Two people didn't want to fight. They were trying to be **peacemakers**.

Two people wanted to fight. They were **troublemakers**.

Make a chart in your book like the one below.

peacemakers	troublemakers

Put the following names on your chart under the correct heading:

Romeo   Tybalt   Benvolio   Mercutio

Death of Mercutio
Key Speeches

(Romeo is trying to make the best of the situation. At first, he doesn't realise how badly Mercutio is wounded. Mercutio is dying. He is very angry. Romeo interfered in his fight with Tybalt.)

ROMEO: Courage, man. The hurt cannot be much.

Be brave – I don't think you're badly hurt.

MERCUTIO: No, 'tis not so deep as a well, nor so wide as a church door. But 'tis enough.
'Twill serve. Ask for me tomorrow, and you shall find me a grave man. I am peppered, I warrant for this world. A plague a' both your houses! Zounds, a dog, a rat, a mouse, a cat, to scratch a man to death! A braggart, a rogue, a villain, that fights by the book of arithmetic! Why the devil came you between us? I was hurt under your arm.

The cut is not as deep as a well or as wide as a church door. But it is bad enough. Anyone who asks for me tomorrow will find me in my grave. I am finished as far as this world goes. A curse on Montagues and Capulets. Scratched to death by a rat, a mouse, a cat. A showoff, a wicked man, that learned to fight from a school book. Why did you get in between us? He wounded me under your arm.

ROMEO: I thought all for the best.

I was just trying to help.

MERCUTIO: Help me into some house, Benvolio,
Or I shall faint. A plague a' both your houses!
They have made worms' meat of me.
I have it, and soundly too. Your houses!

*Help me into a house, Benvolio,
I'm fainting. Curse both your families!
My body will feed the worms.
I am wounded, and I shall die. Your families!*

The Death of Tybalt

With a partner, talk about the following questions. Write the answers in good sentences in your books.
Page 42 in *The Graphic Romeo and Juliet* will help you.

1.   Why was Romeo angry with himself?

2.   Why did Romeo have to run away?

AT 2: 2-5
AT 3: 2-3

RADIO NEWSROOM VERONA

A News Broadcast

You are going to produce a radio news broadcast. You need four people, but you may use more. If possible, tape-record your news broadcast and play it to your own, or another, class. Here are some suggestions to help you to make an interesting broadcast. A script is written for you, but you may wish to write your own.

You will need: a newsreader
a studio technician
an outside broadcaster
an eyewitness[1]

Script for your broadcast

	RADIO VERONA NEWS SCRIPT
NEWSREADER	Good evening. This is the six o'clock news from Radio Newsroom Verona. Trouble has broken out yet again on the streets of Verona. Members of the Montague and the Capulet families were involved in street fights this afternoon. Mercutio, a friend of the Montagues, and Tybalt, a Capulet, were both killed. Romeo, son of Lord and Lady Montague, is accused of killing Tybalt. The Prince, ruler of Verona, has banished Romeo. He must leave the city and never return. We go now to our outside broadcaster in the town square. Rosa Pavarotti, are you there?
OUTSIDE BROADCASTER:	Yes, Mario. Good evening.
NEWSREADER:	Rosa, we're getting reports that the town centre is very quiet tonight. People can't believe the number of killings. They have all gone to their own homes. They are afraid to go outside. Is that true?
OUTSIDE BROADCASTER:	Yes, Mario, that is true. The young men killed this afternoon were well-known men from rich families. How did it happen? That is the question everyone is asking. Also, they are saying, when will the killing stop? And no one has the answer to that question. Everyone is feeling sad and afraid. This is a very bad day for Verona.
NEWSREADER:	Rosa, can we talk to someone who was there this afternoon?
OUTSIDE BROADCASTER:	Yes, indeed, Mario. I have here Signor Martino. He came to the town square soon after the killings.
NEWSREADER:	Signor Martino. Good evening to you and welcome to News at Six. Could you tell us a little bit about what you saw this afternoon?
SIGNOR MARTINO:	Good evening, Mario. Yes indeed, it was terrible here. I was just going for a walk when I heard a noise in the town square. I went to look and there was Tybalt on the ground, covered in blood. Benvolio, a Montague, explained what had happened. As you said, Mario, it was Romeo that killed Tybalt. No one could deny[2] that. Benvolio tried to make excuses because Tybalt had killed Romeo's friend, Mercutio. The Prince said that Romeo had to leave town straight away. If he shows up in Verona again, he's a dead man.
NEWSREADER:	Signor Martino, thank you very much for that eyewitness account, and thank you Rosa Pavarotti, reporting for News at Six. And now the weather news…

You could add some more eyewitness stories. For example, someone might have seen Mercutio dying and heard his angry words. Another eyewitness might talk about Lord and Lady Montague. They would have been very upset when Romeo was sent away forever. Other people might think that Romeo should have been put to death.

[1] eyewitness – someone who saw something with their own eyes
[2] deny – say that something is not true

AT 3: 2-5
AT 1: 2-5

TERRIBLE NEWS

The Nurse returned with terrible news for Juliet. Talk about the questions below with your group or partner. Pages 44 and 45 of your *Graphic Romeo and Juliet* will help you. Answer them in good sentences.

1.   Can you find **two** words that mean, "sent away forever"?

2.   Who was Juliet's cousin?

3.   Why was Juliet angry with Romeo when she first heard about Tybalt?

4.   In the end, did Juliet blame Romeo for the fight?
     (Give a reason for your answer.)

Key Speeches

NURSE: Tybalt is gone, and Romeo banished;
         Romeo that killed him, he is banished.

Tybalt is dead and Romeo has been sent away forever.
Because Romeo killed Tybalt, he has been sent away.

JULIET: O God! Did Romeo's hand shed Tybalt's blood?

O God, did Romeo kill Tybalt?

NURSE: It did, it did! Alas the day, it did!

He did, he did. It's a terrible thing, but he did.

JULIET: O serpent heart, hid with a flowering face!
          Did ever dragon keep so fair a cave?
          Beautiful tyrant! Fiend angelical!
          Dove-feathered raven! Wolvish-ravening lamb!
          O that deceit should dwell
          In such a gorgeous palace!

Oh, heart of a snake hiding behind a nice face.
Did ever an evil beast live in such a nice place.
Beautiful evil man. Devil that looks like an angel.
Ugly black bird all covered in white feathers.
Lamb with the appetite of a wolf.
Oh, that lies should live in a handsome body.

NURSE: Give me some aqua vitae.
         These griefs, these woes, these sorrows make me old.
         Shame come to Romeo!

Give me some brandy,
these terrible things make me feel like an old woman.
Shame on Romeo!

JULIET: Blistered be thy tongue
          For such a wish! He was not born to shame.
          Upon his brow shame is ashamed to sit.
          O, what a beast was I to chide at him!

I hope you get sores on your tongue
for saying such a thing. Shame should not come to Romeo.
He has nothing to be ashamed about.
I was wrong to be angry with him.

NURSE: Will you speak well of him that killed your cousin?

Will you say nice things about the man that killed your cousin?

JULIET: Shall I speak ill of him that is my husband?
          Ah, poor my lord, what tongue shall smooth thy name
          When I, thy three-hours wife have mangled it?
          But wherefore, villain, didst thou kill my cousin?
          That villain cousin would have killed my husband.
          Back, foolish tears, back to your native spring!
          My husband lives that Tybalt would have slain;
          And Tybalt's dead, that would have slain my husband.
          All this is comfort. Wherefore weep I then?

Should I say bad things about the man that is my husband?
Oh, my poor husband, who will speak well of you If I, your wife for only three hours, say bad things about you.
But why, you bad man, did you kill my cousin?
Because that evil cousin would have killed you, my husband.
Silly tears, go back into my eyes!
Tybalt wanted to kill my husband, and my husband is alive;
And Tybalt's dead who wanted to kill my husband.
All this makes me feel better, so why am I crying?

AT 2: 2-5
AT 3: 2-3

— 22 —

FRIAR LAURENCE'S PLAN (1)

> In your groups or with a partner, talk about the questions below. Write the answers in your notebooks. Check each other's work. Have you used good sentences?

1. Where did Romeo go to hide?

2. Who told Romeo about the Prince's punishment?

3. How did Romeo feel?

4. What were two things Romeo should be thankful for?

5. What did the Nurse give to Romeo?

6. The Friar's plan had four parts:
    a) Romeo was to go to a town called _____.

    b) The Friar would send him _____ about Verona.

    c) Soon, the Friar would tell everyone about the _____.

    d) Everyone would be very happy. The Prince would let Romeo _____ _____.

7. Do you think it was a good plan? Give reasons for your answer.

Key Speech

FRIAR LAURENCE:

Go, get thee to thy love, as was decreed.
Ascend her chamber. Hence and comfort her.
But look thou stay not till the Watch be set,
For then thou canst not pass to Mantua,
Where thou shalt live till we can find a time
To blaze your marriage, reconcile your friends,
Beg pardon of the Prince, and call thee back
With twenty hundred times more joy
Than thou wentest forth in lamentation.

Go to Juliet as we decided before, and climb up to her room. Try to cheer her up. Be sure you don't stay until the gates of the town are locked, because if you do, you won't be able to get to Mantua, which is where you must go and live. We will find a good time to tell everyone about your marriage, settle all the quarrels, ask the Prince to let you come back, and bring you home with much more joy and happiness than when you leave at this unhappy time.

AT 2: 2-5
AT 3: 2-4

THE CAPULETS PLANNED A WEDDING

> Talk about the questions below in your groups, or with a partner. Decide the answers
> among yourselves. Tell your answers to the rest of the class. Other people may disagree with you.
> Be ready to give reasons for your answers.

1. What did the County Paris ask the Capulets?

2. What did Lord Capulet do?

3. Was Juliet asked her opinion?

4. What do you think the Capulets should have done?

5. There were two things the Capulets didn't know. If they had known, they would have been very surprised.
   What were the two things they didn't know?

Romeo and Juliet say goodbye
Key Speech

Romeo and Juliet had one precious night together. Juliet didn't want Romeo to leave.
She tried to tell him that it was still night-time, not morning.

JULIET:
Wilt thou be gone? It is not yet near day.
It was the nightingale, and not the lark,
That pierced the fearful hollow of thine ear.
Nightly she sings on yond pomegranate tree.
Believe me, love, it was the nightingale.

Must you go? It isn't daytime yet.
The bird you have just heard was a
nightingale[1]; it wasn't a lark[2],
She sings every night on that tree over
there.
Trust me, darling, it was the nightingale.

[1]nightingale – bird that sings only at night
[2]lark – a bird that usually sings in the early morning

AT 1: 3

A FAMILY ROW

This family row was a big turning point for Juliet. She loved Romeo. She was married to Romeo. Probably for the first time in her life, she disobeyed her parents. Her parents, especially her father, were furious. To test your knowledge of the scene, write the sentences below in your notebooks. Write after each one whether it is *True* or *False*.

True/False

1. Juliet told her mother that she was crying about Tybalt.

2. She was really crying about Mercutio.

3. The wedding was to be in two days' time.

4. Her father said he would throw her out onto the streets.

5. Juliet had always been a troublemaker.

6. The Nurse said that Juliet should marry Paris.

7. That was excellent advice.

8. To marry a second time was against the laws of the church.

9. Juliet thought she would marry Paris.

10. She might have to kill herself.

Key Speeches

JULIET:	Good father, I beseech you on my knees, Hear me with patience but to speak a word.	*Dear father, I beg you on my knees, Please listen to me for a moment; let me say just one word.*
CAPULET:	Hang thee, young baggage! Disobedient wretch! I tell thee what – get thee to church a' Thursday Or never after look me in the face. Speak not, reply not, do not answer me! My fingers itch.	*Get away you young good-for-nothing; you won't do as I say. Be sure you go to the church to be married on Thursday or never see me again. Don't bother to say any more. You deserve to be hit.*

AT 1: 2
AT 2: 2-5

FRIAR LAURENCE'S PLAN (2)

Below is a diagram of Friar Laurence's plan. There were three main steps to the plan. Each step depended on something else happening at the right time. Plans like this can sometimes go wrong! Copy the diagram into your notebook. Then, working with a friend, decide which sentences should go in the "Depends On" column.

Plan	Depends on
Juliet drinks the medicine. She goes to sleep for 42 hours.	
Romeo returns from Mantua to be with Juliet when she wakes.	
Romeo and Juliet go away together.	

Depends on:

1.   Juliet being very brave.

2.   Romeo getting the message that Juliet isn't really dead.

3.   Juliet waking up at the right moment.

THE FRIAR'S MEDICINE

There were good reasons why Juliet was afraid to take the Friar's medicine.
There were other reasons why, in the end, she took it. Working with a partner or in a group, decide
where the reasons belong on the chart below. Copy the chart into your books.

Why Juliet was afraid to take the medicine	Why Juliet drank the medicine

She might really die.

She would wake up in the vault with dead bodies all around her.

She might die from lack of air.

It would be wrong for her to marry Paris.

She might go mad.

She wanted to be with Romeo.

The Friar might be tricking her.

LAMENT FOR JULIET

> Everyone thought Juliet was dead. The Capulets, the Nurse, and Paris were all upset.
> In those days, when someone died, the church bells rang. They rang with one sound, over and over again.
> The bells **tolled**. The speeches below sound like those bells. The sound of the words is more important
> than the meaning. Working in groups of four, practise saying the four speeches in turn, with
> no gaps between the speeches. When you have practised, say the speeches for the rest of the class.

LADY CAPULET: Accursed, unhappy, wretched, hateful day!
Most miserable hour that e'er time saw
In lasting labour of his pilgrimage!
But one, poor one, one poor and loving child,
But one thing to rejoice and solace in,
And cruel death hath catched it from my sight.

NURSE: O woe! O woeful, woeful, woeful day!
Most lamentable day, most woeful day
That ever, ever I did yet behold!
O day, O day, O day! O hateful day!
Never was seen so black a day as this.
O woeful day! O woeful day!

PARIS: Beguiled, divorcèd,[1] wrongèd, spited slain!
Most detestable Death, by thee beguiled,
By cruel, cruel thee quite overthrown.
O love! O life! – Not life, but love in death!

CAPULET: Despised, distressèd, hated, martyred, killed!
Uncomfortable time, why camest thou now
To murder, murder our solemnity?
O child! O child! my soul and not my child!
Dead art thou -- alack, my child is dead,
And with my child my joys are burièd!

[1] Note: where you have the letter e like this è, say the sound of the letter.

AT 2: 4-5

A MESSAGE TO MANTUA

Working in your groups, talk about the questions below. Write the answers in your book. Remember to use good sentences. The class might like to hear some of the different answers to question 5.

BALTHASAR

1. Why did Balthasar ride to Mantua?

2. Why did Romeo ask Balthasar if he had letters from Friar Laurence?

3. What did Romeo decide to do?

4. Why do you think he wanted to buy some poison?

5. You know that Romeo got the wrong message from Balthasar.
    How does it make you feel?

The Friar's plan went wrong

Look back at the chart under "The Friar's Plan (2)" on page 26, Worksheet 4.1. Which part had gone wrong? If you haven't already copied the chart into your notebook, do it now. *The Graphic Romeo and Juliet*, page 66, explains why the plan went wrong. In your notebooks, write the answers to the questions below.

1. Friar Laurence sent a letter to Romeo saying that Juliet wasn't really _____ .

2. He gave the letter to a man named _____ _____ .

3. Friar Laurence got very _____ .

4. Romeo had not received his _____ .

5. Friar Laurence went to the _____ .

AT 3: 2-4

THE CAPULET'S VAULT

> In the end, things happened very quickly. Friar Laurence's plan went wrong.
> Everything was against Romeo and Juliet. Working with a partner, look at the following sentences and arrange them in the correct order. Write them in your notebooks.

Romeo dragged Paris's body into the vault.

Friar Laurence came along.

Juliet took Romeo's dagger and killed herself.

Paris tried to stop Romeo going into the vault.

Juliet heard the night watchman coming.

Romeo didn't know Juliet was only sleeping and would soon wake up.

Friar Laurence wanted Juliet to leave the vault with him.

Romeo kissed Juliet goodbye and took the poison.

Romeo thought Juliet looked very beautiful, lying in the vault.

Juliet refused to leave the vault with Friar Laurence.

The end of the fighting

> Friar Laurence explained to the Prince and all the people what had happened to Romeo and Juliet. His story is below, written in modern English. Fill in the spaces, then read it aloud. Other members of the class will be the Capulets, Old Montague, the Prince, and people of the town. The Friar tells his story. It is very sad. The other people should show their feelings.

"Well, you see, Romeo was Juliet's _____ , and she was his _____ . I married them.

The very day they were married, was the day that Romeo _____ Tybalt. Romeo, newly married, was sent

away from _____ . Juliet was _____ for Romeo, not for Tybalt. You, her parents, were

_____ her to marry Paris. She came to me saying she wanted to _____ herself. I gave her a sleeping

potion that would make her look as if she was _____ . I sent a _____ to Romeo telling him to come

back and take Juliet away. My messenger, Friar John, didn't get to _____ . He brought my letter back.

I was _____ about what would happen to Juliet when she woke up alone. I came to get her.

When I came, _____ and Romeo were both here, dead. Juliet woke, and I asked her to _____ with me.

We heard a _____ , and I left. Now she has killed herself.

If any of this has been my _____ , I offer you my _____."

> husband   wife   killed   Verona   crying   forcing   killed   dead
> letter   Mantua   worried   Paris   leave   noise   fault   life

> From the headlines below, choose the two that best fit the ending of the story. Paste or copy them into your notebook. Write a newspaper story to go with one of your headlines.

"THERE WILL NEVER BE PEACE!" SAY THE TWO FAMILIES

MONTAGUES AND CAPULETS: PEACE AT LAST

ROMEO AND JULIET: TOGETHER IN DEATH

"I'LL BUILD A STATUE OF JULIET!" SAYS MONTAGUE

"I SHOULD HAVE BEEN MORE FIRM!" PRINCE

MAKING THE AUDIENCE LISTEN

Romeo and Juliet has two things to make the audience sit up and pay attention. The first scene is a street fight. That is a good beginning with plenty of action. Even before the street fight, there is a **prologue**. **What is the prologue?**

The prologue is a speech made by an actor or actress **before the play begins**. The prologue tells the people what the play will be about. It should make the people want to find out what happens in the play.

Here is the prologue to *Romeo and Juliet* written in modern English, then in Shakespeare's English. The prologue can be divided into four parts. Read it first in modern English, then in Shakespeare's English. Try to read it so that your listeners can understand the meaning.

The Prologue

> *Two families, both respected, live in Verona, where our play takes place.*
> *The families had a row many years ago, and fighting has started again.*
> *One group is fighting another group. This is called civil war.*

> *These two enemy families gave birth to two lovers, who have the stars against them from the start.*
> *Everything goes wrong for the lovers, but their deaths made their parents end the fighting.*

> *This two hour play will be about the sad story of their love which ended in death, and the fighting*
> *between the families, which only the death of their children finally ends.*

> *If you listen carefully, our acting and our play will show you the whole story.*

The Prologue

> Two households, both alike in dignity
> In fair Verona, where we lay our scene,
> From ancient grudge break to new mutiny,
> Where civil blood makes civil hands unclean.

> From forth the fatal loins of these two foes
> A pair of star-crossed lovers take their life;
> Whose misadventured piteous overthrows
> Doth with their death bury their parents' strife.

> The fearful passage of their death-marked love
> And the continuance of their parents' rage,
> Which, but their children's end, naught could remove,
> Is now the two hours traffic of our stage.

> The which if you with patient ears attend,
> What here shall miss, our toil shall strive to mend.

AT 2: 3-5

EVERYONE JOINS THE FIGHT

For this scene, you will need a lot of actors. Sampson and Gregory (Capulets), Abram and another servant (Montagues) are already fighting. Benvolio has been watching them. You will also need Tybalt, old Capulet, Lady Capulet, old Montague, Lord Montague, and four people of the town, as well as the Prince at the very end.

Things to remember:

1. The space in your classroom that you are using for the stage will have to be quite big.
2. The speeches are said clearly and quite quickly, with no gaps between the speeches. One should follow quickly after another.
3 These people are angry. They can shout if they feel like it.
4. They will be waving their swords and weapons. There should be lots of movement.

(Benvolio watches the fighting. He takes out his sword and rushes between the others.)

| BENVOLIO: | Part, fools!
Put up your swords. You know not what you do. | *Stop it, you fools.* |

(Tybalt comes in and sneaks up behind Benvolio. He shouts at Benvolio, making him jump.)

| TYBALT: | What, are thou drawn among these heartless hinds?
Turn thee, Benvolio, look upon thy death. | *Why are you fighting with a bunch of servants?*
Turn around, Benvolio, I'm going to kill you. |

| BENVOLIO: | I do but keep the peace. Put up thy sword,
Or manage it to part these men with me. | *I'm trying to stop the fight. Put your sword away or use it to help me.* |

| TYBALT: | What, drawn, and talk of peace? I hate the word
As I hate hell, all Montagues, and thee.
Have at thee coward. | *How can you have your sword out and talk about peace? I hate that word and I hate hell and I hate all the Montagues and I hate you. Fight, you coward!* |

(Benvolio and Tybalt fight. Three or four people of the town now enter with weapons, clubs, pikes, etc. They join in the fighting. They shout as they push and shove each other.)

| FIRST CITIZEN: | Strike! |

| SECOND CITIZEN: | Beat them down! |

| THIRD CITIZEN: | Down with the Capulets! |

| FOURTH CITIZEN: | Down with the Montagues! |

(Old Capulet and Lady Capulet come rushing in. Old Capulet is a bit shaky on his legs.)

| CAPULET: | What noise is this? Give me my long sword, ho! |

| LADY CAPULET: | A crutch, a crutch! Why call you for a sword? | *A walking stick is what you need. Why are you shouting for a sword?* |

(Old Montague and his wife rush in. Old Montague is waving a sword.)

| CAPULET: (shouting) | My sword, I say. Old Montague is come
And flourishes his blade in spite of me. | *And is waving his sword to show me up.* |

| MONTAGUE: | Thou villain Capulet! --Hold me not. Let me go. |

| LADY MONTAGUE: | Thou shall not stir one foot to seek a foe. | *You will not go looking for a fight.* |

(At this point, the Prince enters and they all freeze as they are.)

THE BALCONY SCENE

Shakespeare's English	*Modern English*

ROMEO: See how she leans her cheek upon her hand!
O that I were a glove upon that hand,
That I might touch that cheek.

*Look, she's resting her cheek on her hand!
If I could only be a glove on her hand
I would be able to touch her cheek!*

JULIET: O Romeo, Romeo! – wherefore art thou Romeo?
Deny thy father and refuse thy name.
Or, if thou wilt not, be but sworn my love,
And I'll no longer be a Capulet.

*O Romeo, Romeo! Why are you called Romeo?
If only you could say that you are not your
father's son, and change your name.
Or, if you don't want to do that, if you promise to
love me,
I will change my name, and not be a Capulet any
more.*

ROMEO: Call me but love, and I'll be new baptised.
Henceforth, I never will be Romeo.

*I'll take you at your word.
If you love me, I'll be baptised again.
From now on I shan't be Romeo any more.*

JULIET: What man art thou that, thus bescreened in night,
So stumblest on my counsel?

*Who are you, hiding in the darkness,
listening to what I've been saying?*

ROMEO: By a name
I know not how to tell thee who I am.
My name, dear saint, is hateful to myself,
Because it is an enemy to thee.
Had I it written, I would tear the word.

*I don't know how to tell you my name.
I hate my name
because it makes me your enemy
If it were written on a piece of paper, I would rip
it up.*

JULIET: My ears have not yet drunk a hundred words
Of thy tongue's uttering, yet I know the sound,
Art thou not Romeo, and a Montague?

*I haven't heard you speak even a hundred words
Yet I know the sound of your voice.
Aren't you Romeo, and a member of the
Montague family?*

ROMEO: Neither, fair maid, if either thee dislike.

*I won't be either Romeo or a Montague if you
don't like those names.*

JULIET: Three words, dear Romeo, and good night indeed.
If that thy bent of love be honourable,
Thy purpose marriage, send me word tomorrow,
By one that I'll procure to come to thee,
Where and what time thou wilt perform the rite,
And all my fortunes at thy foot I'll lay
And follow thee my lord throughout the world.
(Pause for a moment) What o'clock tomorrow
Shall I send to thee?

*A few more words, dear Romeo, then we really
have to say goodnight.
If you truly love me
and want to marry me, I will send someone to
you tomorrow
to find out where and when we can be married,
then I will belong to you
and I will follow you wherever you go in the
world.
(Pause for a moment) What time tomorrow
shall I send someone to you?*

ROMEO: By the hour of nine.

By nine o'clock in the morning.

JULIET: Good night, goodnight! Parting is such sweet sorrow
That I shall say goodnight till it be morrow.

*Good night, goodnight! It's very sad to say
goodnight
But we know we'll see each other again
tomorrow.*

ROMEO: Sleep dwell upon thine eyes, peace in thy breast!
Would I were sleep and peace, so sweet to rest!
Hence will I to my ghostly Friar's cell,
His help to crave and my dear hap to tell.

*Sleep will come to your eyes, peace will come to
your breast!
I wish I were "sleep" and "peace" to be in such
beautiful places!
Now I'm going to see the Friar,
I'll tell him everything that has happened and ask
for his help.*

THE NURSE WAS SLOW TO GIVE THE MESSAGES

Key Speeches

> Look at the picture on page 35 of *The Graphic Romeo and Juliet*. The Nurse returns from getting the rope ladder. She is hot and tired and flops down in a chair. She quite enjoys her power over Juliet at this moment. She has the messages. Juliet wants the messages. The Nurse takes her time. Juliet gets wound up.

JULIET: O God, she comes! O honey Nurse, what news?
Hast thou met with him?
Now, good sweet Nurse – O Lord, why lookest thou sad?
Though news be sad, yet tell them merrily.
If good, thou shamest the music of sweet news
By playing it to me with a sour face.

*Oh, here she is! Oh, dear Nurse, what news?
Have you met with him?
Now, good, dear Nurse – why are you looking sad?
If you have sad news, still tell it cheerfully.
If it's good news, you'll still spoil it for me if you tell it with such a sad face.*

NURSE: I am aweary. Give me leave a while.
Fie, how my bones ache! What a jaunce have I!

*I'm tired. Leave me alone for a minute.
My bones hurt. What a walk I had!*

JULIET: I would thou hadst my bones, and I thy news.
Nay, come, I pray thee speak. Good, good Nurse, speak.

I'd be happy for you to have my bones, if I could have your news. Come, please speak. Good, good Nurse, speak.

NURSE: Jesu, what haste! Can you not stay a while?
Do you not see that I am out of breath?

Heavens, what a hurry! Can't you wait a minute? Can't you tell that I'm out of breath?

JULIET: How art thou out of breath when thou has breath
To say to me that thou art out of breath?
The excuse that thou dost make in this delay
Is longer than the tale thou dost excuse.
Is thy news good or bad? Answer to that.
Say either, and I'll stay the circumstance.
Let me be satisfied, is't good or bad?

*How can you be out of breath when you're using your breath to tell me that you're out of breath?
You're taking longer making excuses than you would take to tell me the news.
Is the news good or bad? Just tell me that.
Just say which it is, and I'll hear the details later. Now tell me, is it good or bad?*

ROMEO – A "WANTED" POSTER

The Prince said that Romeo had to leave Verona. He was banished for murdering Tybalt. If Romeo was seen in Verona again, he would be put to death. The people needed to know what he looked like, and what to do if they saw him.

Design a poster with a picture of Romeo. You could choose one of the pictures of Romeo in *The Graphic Shakespeare*, or you could draw your own. An example is given below to help you.

IF YOU SEE THIS MAN:

GO AT ONCE TO THE PALACE AND
REPORT TO THE PRINCE
NOTE: ROMEO IS CONSIDERED DANGEROUS!

MEDICINE MEN

Here is what Romeo said to the Apothecary after buying the poison:

ROMEO: Here is thy gold, worse poison to men's souls,
          Doing more murder in this loathsome world,
          Than these poor compounds that thou mayst
          not sell.
          I sell thee poison, thou hast sold me none.
          Farewell, buy food, and get thyself in flesh.

Here is your money, which is more harmful to people's spirits,
and causes the death of more people in this nasty world
than these pathetic mixtures that you are not allowed to sell.
I am giving you poison, you didn't sell me any.
Goodbye, buy yourself some food and get a bit fatter.

To Romeo, what was the worst poison? Do you agree with Romeo?

Write a sentence that begins:

I agree with Romeo because _____ .

or

I disagree with Romeo because _____ .

FRIAR LAURENCE

THE APOTHECARY

Working in groups or with a partner, look at the pictures of Friar Laurence and the Apothecary.
Cut out or draw the pictures in your notebook. Talk about the following questions and write the answers
in good sentences. Read your answers to the class.

1.   Why did Friar Laurence give Juliet the sleeping potion?

2.   Why did the Apothecary let Romeo have the poison?

3.   What did Friar Laurence use to make his medicines?

4.   Whose medicine would you rather take, the Friar's or the Apothecary's?

The 'Who am I?' Game

You need 5 activity sheets for this game, including this one. Prepare for the 'Who Am I' game as follows:

1.   Paste each set of character clues onto a separate card.

2.   Add the appropriate portrait from the Picture Gallery.

3.   Number the cards, the order is not important and write the names and numbers on a master sheet. (for example: 1. Romeo   2. Juliet   3. The Nurse   etc).

4.   Make up individual score cards as shown below.

NAME:		
CARD No.	POINTS SCORED	TOTAL
	GRAND TOTAL	

Rules of the Game

1.   Working in pairs, one student holds the card with the blank side facing the partner. The partner asks questions that can be answered '*Yes*' or '*No*'.

>   For example: '*Are you a man?*'
>   '*Do you enjoy fighting?*'

2.   Each question counts as one point.

3.   Each direct question about the name of a character counts 5 points if the answer is '*No*'.
       For example: '*Are you Lady Capulet?*' counts 5 points if the answer is no. This is to stop you simply guessing, hoping to get lucky!

4.   Clues may be offered, one at a time, in return for a small 'price' of two points.
       At the request, '*Please give me a clue*', one of the clues on the card is read out, and two points are added to the score.

5.   Mark the points on your score card as you go along. Add up the points on each line for the 'Total' column as you identify each character.

Take turns holding the cards and asking the questions. Remember, the aim is to guess the name of the character while getting the **lowest** number of points.

CHARACTER CLUES •1

Romeo Paste portrait here	> I thought I could never love anyone but Rosaline. > I helped a servant read the list of guests for the Capulets' party. > It was my fault that Mercutio was killed. > I married Juliet. > I climbed to Juliet's bedroom with a rope ladder. > I killed Tybalt. > I had to go away to Mantua.

Juliet Paste portrait here	> At the time of the story, I was fourteen years old. > I have had a Nurse since I was very young. > Paris wanted to marry me. > Friar Laurence gave me a sleeping potion. > My husband killed my cousin. > My parents had a lovely party for me. > I didn't want to live without Romeo. > My marriage had to be kept secret.

Benvolio Paste portrait here	> I was Romeo's cousin. > I always tried to stop fights. > I worried about Romeo when he seemed unhappy. > I told Romeo to get away after he killed Tybalt. > I persuaded Romeo to go to the Capulets' party. > Romeo thought he was in love with Rosaline. > I said he should meet other girls.

Lady Montague Paste portrait here	> My husband and I were worried about our son. > I tried to stop my husband fighting with Old Capulet. > My son was banished from Verona. I became ill.

CHARACTER CLUES • 2

Tybalt Paste portrait here	> I hated the Montagues. > I loved fighting. > I didn't like the idea of peace. > I recognised Romeo at the party. > I wanted to have a fight with Romeo at the party. > Old Capulet wouldn't let me fight Romeo at the party. > I was going to fight Romeo, sooner or later. > I killed that cheeky Mercutio.
Mercutio Paste portrait here	> I enjoyed life. I loved a joke. > I tried to cheer up Romeo. > I told Romeo not to take love so seriously. > I called Tybalt "King of Cats"! > It was Romeo's fault that I got killed.
The Nurse Paste portrait here	> I had looked after Juliet since she was a little girl. > Juliet gave me a ring to give to Romeo. > I collected the rope ladder and took it to Juliet. > I thought Lord Capulet was too hard on Juliet. > I found Juliet's body, on the morning of her wedding day.
The Friar Paste portrait here	> I knew all about plants and medicines. > I could see that Romeo and Juliet were very much in love. > I wanted the Montagues and the Capulets to end their fighting. > I married Romeo and Juliet. > Romeo came to me when he was in trouble. > I gave Juliet a sleeping potion. > My messenger didn't get to Mantua. > My plans went wrong. It wasn't my fault.
Prince Escalus Paste portrait here	> I was sick and tired of all the fighting. > The next person to start a fight would die. > I sent Romeo away from Verona. > I was the ruler of Verona.

CHARACTER CLUES • 3

Old Capulet

Paste portrait here

> I put on a big party for my daughter.
> I thought Paris would be a good husband for my daughter.
> I had a row with Tybalt at the party.
> I was furious with Juliet. She didn't want to marry Paris.
> I saw Romeo, a Montague, at the party. I didn't want to make a fuss.
> Montague and I knew we had to end the fighting.

Lady Capulet

Paste portrait here

> I tried to stop my husband fighting with Old Montague.
> I asked Juliet if she could love the County Paris.
> Juliet always did as we told her.
> My husband and I were very angry when Juliet refused to marry Paris.
> My husband and I were very happy when Juliet said she would marry Paris.
> My beautiful daughter killed herself.

Old Montague

Paste portrait here

> I wanted to fight Old Capulet. My wife tried to stop me.
> I was the head of the Montague family.
> My wife died of grief.
> My son was banished for killing Tybalt.
> I said I would put up a gold statue of Juliet.

Paris

Paste portrait here

> I really wanted to marry Juliet.
> Twice, I asked to marry Juliet.
> I was overjoyed when Old Capulet said we could be married.
> Juliet was found dead on the morning of our wedding.

The Apothecary

Paste portrait here

> I sold a young man some very strong poison.
> It was against the law to sell poison in Mantua. I was paid a lot of money for it.
> I was very poor. I needed the money.

PORTRAIT GALLERY

Cut around dotted lines and paste portraits on to the character clue cards.

Romeo

Juliet

Benvolio

Tybalt

Old Capulet

Lady Capulet

Old Montague

Lady Montague

Paris

Nurse

Mercutio

Prince Escalus

Friar Laurence

Apothecary

DESKTOP TEACHING

To the teacher: This is a whole-class exercise to make sure that everyone understands the main points of the play. First, distribute these 'Desktop Teacher' cards to students who are sure they can answer the questions.

The students who have the "Desktop Teacher" cards put them on their desks so that the questions can be clearly seen. Everyone first tries to answer the questions themselves, using the Answer Sheet on page 44. If they are not sure about an answer, they visit the 'Desktop Teacher' who will explain it. By moving from Desktop to Desktop, everyone should end up with a good understanding of the main points of the play.

Why were the Montagues and the Capulets fighting? Who got involved?

Who was the Prince? What did he do?

Why was Romeo banished?

Why did Old Capulet tell Tybalt to leave Juliet's party?

Give three examples of times when Tybalt wanted to start a fight.

DESKTOP TEACHING (continued)

Give three examples of times when Friar Laurence tried to help Romeo and Juliet.

Why did Juliet have a terrible row with her parents?

What was Friar Laurence's sleeping potion supposed to do?

Did Balthasar help to cause Romeo's death?

How did Romeo help to cause Mercutio's death?

DESKTOP TEACHING (continued)

Answer Sheet

NAME:_____   Form:_____

1. Why were the Montagues and the Capulets fighting? Who got involved?

    _____
    _____
    _____

2. Who was the Prince? What did he do? _____

    _____
    _____

3. Why was Romeo banished? _____

    _____
    _____

4. Why did Old Capulet tell Tybalt to leave Juliet's party? _____

    _____
    _____

5. Give three examples of when Tybalt wanted to start a fight:
    i) _____
    ii) _____
    iii) _____

6. Give three examples of when Friar Laurence tried to help Romeo and Juliet:
    i) _____
    ii) _____
    iii) _____

7. Why did Juliet have a terrible row with her parents? _____

    _____
    _____

8. What was Friar Laurence's sleeping potion supposed to do? _____

    _____

9. Did Balthasar help to cause Romeo's death? _____

    _____

10. How did Romeo help to cause Mercutio's death? _____

    _____

SHAKESPEARE'S THEATRE

What were theatres like when Shakespeare wrote his plays?
The theatres were eight-sided, with covered seats all around and the middle part open to the sky. Remember there was no electricity, so it was important to have daylight.

Those who could pay more for their seats sat in the covered part. Poorer people stood on the ground around the stage. Because they stood on the ground, they were called **groundlings**. The groundlings were often young apprentices – boys learning a trade such as making shoes, gloves, or clothes. They had very little money.

Before the play started, and while it was going on, the people in the theatre were talking, eating, and drinking. It was very important that the beginning of the play made the people want to keep quiet, listen, and pay attention to the play.

Who's Who?

Cut out the pictures of the characters below. They are: *Romeo, Juliet, Benvolio, Tybalt, Old Capulet, Mercutio, Nurse, Friar Laurence.* **Paste them into your notebook with a few lines between each one.**

Here are some things that the people might say about themselves. Can you match the sentences with the right faces? Write the sentences underneath the faces.

> *Romeo was my cousin and my friend.*
>
> *How I hated all the Montagues!*
>
> *I tried to tell Romeo that being in love was fun.*
>
> *Once, I was in love with Rosaline.*
>
> *I love my garden.*
>
> *Paris wants to marry me.*
>
> *I put on a big party for my daughter.*
>
> *I have worked for the Capulets since Juliet was a baby.*
>
> *When I saw Juliet, I fell in love – forever.*
>
> *I was on the balcony, speaking aloud. Romeo heard me!*
>
> *I wanted Romeo and Juliet to be married, to end the fighting.*
>
> *I recognised Romeo at the party. We should have thrown him out.*
>
> *I told Paris that he could marry Juliet.*
>
> *I gave Juliet a special sleeping potion.*
>
> *I told Romeo that we should go to the Capulets' party.*
>
> *Juliet gave me a ring to take to Romeo.*

Can you make up some more sentences like these and write them under the pictures? Talk about your ideas with a partner.

Romeo

Juliet

Benvolio

Tybalt

Old Capulet

Mercutio

Nurse

Friar Laurence

ROMEO & JULIET
RECORD OF MY WORK

Name: _____

Date started: _____

Form: _____

Date completed: _____

TITLE AND NUMBER OF ACTIVITY	How well did you do this activity?			Was it easy or difficult?			TEACHER'S OR PUPIL'S COMMENTS
	Very Well	Quite Well	I could have tried harder	Too difficult	Too easy	Just right	

WHAT THINGS HAVE I IMPROVED?

Writing in sentences	
Using full stops and capital letters	
Spelling	
Understanding Shakespeare's English	
Acting and speaking Shakespeare's English	
What did I enjoy about *Romeo and Juliet*?	
What went well with my work?	
How can I do better?	